Rita
the Rollerskating Fairy

Join the **Rainbow Magic Reading Challenge!**

Read the story and collect your fairy points to climb the
k.

To Erik

Special thanks to
Rachel Elliot

ORCHARD BOOKS

First published in Great Britain in 2019 by The Watts Publishing Group

1 3 5 7 9 10 8 6 4 2

© 2019 Rainbow Magic Limited.
© 2019 HIT Entertainment Limited.
Illustrations © Orchard Books 2019

HIT entertainment

The moral rights of the author and illustrator have been asserted.

A CIP catalogue record for this book is available from the British Library.

ISBN 978 1 40835 524 4

Printed and bound in Great Britain by Clays Ltd, Elcograf S.p.A.

MIX
Paper from
responsible sources
FSC
www.fsc.org
FSC® C104740

The paper and board used in this book are made from wood from responsible sources

Orchard Books
An imprint of Hachette Children's Group
Part of The Watts Publishing Group Limited
Carmelite House, 50 Victoria Embankment, London EC4Y 0DZ

An Hachette UK Company
www.hachette.co.uk
www.hachettechildrens.co.uk

Rita
the Rollerskating
Fairy

By Daisy Meadows

ORCHARD

www.rainbowmagicbooks.co.uk

The Fairyland Palace

Fairy Arena

Tippington Town

Cool Kids Leisure Centre

Jack Frost's Ice Castle

Wetherbury Village

Jack Frost's Spell

I must get strong! I'll start today.
But kids are getting in my way.
They jump and run, they spin and bound.
I can't do sports with them around!

Goblins, ruin every club.
Spoil their sports and make them blub.
I'll prove it's true, for all to see:
My sister's not as strong as me!

Contents

Chapter One
Lemons

"I love the Cool Kids Leisure Centre," said Kirsty Tate.

She held out her arms and twirled around in the middle of the foyer.

"Me too," said her best friend, Rachel Walker. "I'm so glad it opened halfway between Tippington and Wetherbury. It's brilliant that we get to choose an after-school club together."

Lucy, the lady who was organising the after-school sports clubs, looked up as they walked over to her.

"How was the bike club?" she asked.

"It was even more exciting than we expected," said Kirsty, sharing a secret smile with Rachel.

With the help of Bonnie the Bike-Riding Fairy, Rachel and Kirsty had chased a cycling goblin around the countryside, ridden a raft down a rushing river and rescued Bonnie's magical bracelet. As friends of Fairyland, they were used to enchanted adventures. But their adventure with Bonnie had been one of the most exciting yet.

"I'm very glad to hear that you

had fun at the bike club," said Lucy. "There are two other clubs running this afternoon. Would you like to try rollerskating next?"

"That would be great," said Rachel. "I love rollerskating."

"The teacher, Liz, has set up in hall two," said Lucy. "She'll fit you with a pair

of rollerskates each."

Rachel and Kirsty thanked her and hurried towards hall two. They opened the door and met a blast of pop music and laughter. Rollerskaters were skidding slowly across the room. Their arms were held out wide and their legs wobbled.

"Hi, and welcome to Rollerskating Club," said a young woman with long, dark hair. "I'm Liz. I can't wait to get you started. Rollerskating is great fun and a fantastic way to keep fit."

The girls told her their names and she went to get them some skates. Rachel and Kirsty shared a worried look.

"I hope that Jack Frost doesn't cause trouble for this club," said Kirsty. "He's already made the bikes break and the trampolines collapse."

"I keep thinking about that too," said Rachel. "Keep a lookout for goblins."

Jack Frost had stolen four of the magical bracelets that belonged to the After-School Sports Fairies. There were still two left to find. Jack Frost wanted to stop people from using the leisure centre so that he could get fit without anyone watching him. Then he was planning to win an arm-wrestling match against his sister Jilly Chilly.

"Here we are," said Liz, coming back with some skates. "I think this is going to be a popular club. Lots of people asked about it after they heard that the roller derby was coming to the city stadium."

"I heard about that," said Kirsty. "It sounds amazing. All the best rollerskaters in the country are going to be there."

"Yes, showing off all their best moves and tricks," said Liz. "I've got tickets to see Cara White tomorrow. She's the world champion."

CRASH! There was a yell from behind them as two girls skated into each other. They landed on the floor and pulled themselves to the side.

"This is why it's a great idea for everyone to skate in the same direction," said Liz, helping them up.

"That's what's so strange – we *were* skating in the same direction," said the first girl, rubbing her shin. "I don't know what happened."

"I lost control," said the second girl. "I must have spun around."

Just then, a boy called from across the hall.

"Liz, where did you put the kneepads?"

"They're in the red bag, Rob," said Liz. The boy shook his head.

"The red bag's empty," he said.

Rachel and Kirsty exchanged a worried glance.

"The crashes and missing equipment

must be happening because Jack Frost
has stolen the After-School Sports Fairies'
magic bracelets," said Kirsty. "He's
making everything go wrong so that he
can have the leisure centre to himself."

"It won't work," said Rachel in a
determined voice. "Not if we have
anything to do with it."

"Girls, would you help Rob look for
the kneepads before you put your skates
on?" Liz asked them. "I want everyone to

wear them before they start rollerskating fast."

Rachel and Kirsty hurried over to the back of the hall, while Liz called all the other skaters together.

"Let's start with the basics," she said. "Can anyone tell me what a lemon is?"

"A fruit," called out several voices.

"Yes – and no," said Liz with a laugh. "When it comes to rollerskating, I want you to try a completely different sort of lemon. It's an exercise to help you get some control. We're going to keep our skates on the floor and just roll forwards slowly, moving our feet together and apart, together and apart."

As Rachel and Kirsty started searching for the kneepads, the class began practising their lemons.

"I'm looking forward to trying that," said Kirsty.

She reached out to an orange bag, and then let out a little cry of surprise.

"Rachel, this bag is glowing," she whispered. "My heart is thumping like mad. It must be a fairy!"

Chapter Two
Back to Fairyland

Kirsty unzipped the orange bag and saw Rita the Rollerskating Fairy waving up at them.

"Hi, Rita!" they said together.

Rita was wearing a flowery blouse that tied at the waist, with a matching pair of rollerskates and a flippy red skirt.

"Hello, Rachel and Kirsty," she replied, flicking back her wavy white-blonde hair. "I've come to ask for your help. There's a problem at the Fairyland Skatepark. Please will you come with me and help to sort it out?"

"Of course we will," said Rachel at once. "But how can you magic us away? Liz and the others are busy practising, but Rob is bound to notice two people disappearing."

Rita peeped out of the bag and looked at Rob over the top of her glasses.

"Hmm," she said. "We just need to

make him look in the opposite direction."

She waved her wand, and the girls saw something sparkling in the corner. Rob noticed it too, and walked towards the corner to investigate.

"This is your chance," said Rita. "Come closer."

"But the bag's not big enough," said Kirsty.

"Trust me," said Rita, smiling.

Rachel and Kirsty bent down to look into the bag. And instead of bumping into each other or the floor, they just kept going deeper.

"Oh my goodness, we're all the way inside the bag," said Rachel.

There was a flicker of silvery sparkles and the girls felt their skin tingle. They blinked, trying to get used to the half-light. Then they looked at each other and felt a rush of excitement.

"Rachel, we're fairies," Kirsty whispered.

A faint glimmer of fairy dust hung in the air around them. Then Rita skated out of the darkness, looped around and stopped in front of them.

"Thank you for saying you'll help," she said, hugging them.

"Are we still inside the bag?" Kirsty asked, peering into the shadows.

"Yes, but not for long," said Rita.

Her eyes twinkled and she waved her wand. Red rollerskates appeared on Rachel's feet, while Kirsty found that she had purple ones. Then the floor of the bag arched up under their feet. It turned into a slope that got steeper and steeper. Then they started to roll down it.

"Wheee!" Rachel squealed.

Faster and faster, one after the other, the fairies zoomed down the slope of the bag.

"What if we hit the side of the bag?" Kirsty cried.

"Don't worry," said Rita, swerving into the lead.

She pointed her wand at the side of the bag, and it drew the shape of a golden

door. The door opened and the fairies whizzed out . . . but not into the hall. They were rollerskating under a blue sky full of puffy white clouds. There were green hills on either side, dotted with toadstool houses.

"Welcome to the Fairyland Skatepark," said Rita.

She spun around with her arms stretched out wide. Rachel and Kirsty stared in amazement. The bag had completely vanished, and they were in the middle of the biggest skatepark they had ever seen. There were ramps, rails and halfpipes everywhere they looked.

"Wow, this place is amazing," said Rachel. "But where are all the fairies? Why isn't the park filled with skaters?"

"I think I know," said Kirsty, staring at

something over Rachel's left shoulder. "It's filled with goblins instead!"

Rachel whirled around. A gaggle of goblins was rushing towards them. Every single one of them was on skateboards.

"Oh my goodness, they're incredible," Rachel cried.

"They're running wild," said Rita. "They won't listen to me, and they've already pulled up some plants and damaged the rails. I don't know how to stop them."

"Look at all the litter," said Kirsty.

The goblins had thrown sweet wrappers and screwed-up crisp packets all over the skatepark.

"Stop!" exclaimed the fairies.

The goblins cackled with laughter and whizzed past them, leaping and twirling into the air.

"How can they be so good?" said Rita.

She sped after the goblins, and they scattered in all directions. The fairies chased them.

"Come back!" called Rachel.

"Please come back and pick up your litter," Kirsty added.

"It's getting too boring around here," yelled a long-legged goblin. "Let's go to Goblin Grotto and chase everyone!"

The goblins squawked and cheered. The

long-legged goblin held one hand in the air.

"Follow me!" he exclaimed.

"There's something glittering on his wrist," said Rita. "Oh, Rachel, Kirsty . . . it's my magical bracelet!"

Chapter Three
Skatepark Scoundrels

"Don't let them get away!" Kirsty cried. "We have to follow them to Goblin Grotto and get that bracelet back."

In single file, the goblins hurtled along the bank of a winding river. They whizzed across a bridge and leapt over logs and fallen branches. Behind them,

Rachel, Kirsty and Rita were struggling to keep up. They wobbled and skidded. Their legs shook and they kept falling over.

"This is all because the goblins have got my magical bracelet," said Rita.

"Without it, rollerskating clubs and groups everywhere will struggle to skate in a straight line. It's time to use our wings."

With a quick flutter of her wings, her wheels left the ground. Rachel and Kirsty did the same. The goblins were just a speck in the distance, but now it would be easier to catch them up.

"It's getting colder," said Rachel. "We must be getting close to Goblin Grotto."

The goblin village was close to Jack Frost's castle, in the greyest corner of Fairyland. The fairies shivered as they got closer to the goblins. A mass of snow clouds had gathered above, and they were flying above deep snowdrifts. The green hills around them turned into steep ice mountains.

"Woohoo!" the goblins cheered.
"Welcome home!"

They whooped as they swept down a
steep slope towards the huts of Goblin
Grotto.

"They're going too fast!" Rita cried.

The green rollerskaters hurtled into
the village. Above, Rachel, Kirsty and

Rita could do nothing to stop them. The narrow streets were plunged into chaos. Goblin families dived into doorways and alleys to escape. One of the wild rollerskaters zoomed into a washing line and got it tangled around his waist. He dragged it with him, pulling a string of green clothes behind him like the tail of a kite.

"Where's the goblin with the bracelet?" Rachel called. "He's the one we have to talk to."

It was hard to tell who was who. There were rollerskaters everywhere. Some were trying out their skating tricks and balancing on each other's shoulders. Then one goblin crashed into the wall of a hut. Screeching, a second goblin tripped and sent many others tumbling on to the ground.

"Poor things, I hope they're not hurt," said Kirsty, looking at the jumble of arms, legs and rollerskates.

"It's odd that they crashed," said Rachel in a thoughtful voice. "They've been skating so perfectly up till now. It's almost as if the magic of the bracelet wasn't with them any more."

Kirsty gazed around and clapped her hands together in excitement.

"Rachel, you're right," she said. "Look over there."

A rollerskater goblin was standing still in the middle of the village's main square. The fairies landed in front of him. They could see Rita's magical bracelet dangling from his wrist.

"Why have you stopped?" Kirsty asked.

"I don't want to skate around the silly village all day," snapped the goblin.

"What do you want?" asked Rachel, taking a step forward. "Maybe we can help . . . if you give that bracelet back to Rita."

The goblin's eyes glittered with naughtiness.

"I want to do something more than break a few washing lines," he said. "I wish that I could go and get the ultimate rollerskating thrill."

There was a flash of golden light, then a flurry of sparkles, and the goblin had vanished. Rita put her hand to her mouth in alarm, and Rachel and Kirsty gasped.

"Where did he go?" they cried.

"It's the power of my bracelet," said Rita with a groan. "It granted the goblin's wish, and he has gone to be part of the ultimate rollerskating thrill."

"What is the ultimate rollerskating thrill?" asked Rachel.

"It's the roller derby," Rita whispered. "The goblin has gone to join in!"

Chapter Four
The Ultimate Rollerskating Thrill

"We have to get there and stop him before he spoils it for everyone," said Kirsty.

Rita nodded and waved her wand. A shooting star appeared, pulling a stripe of rainbow colours behind it. Rita flew up and landed on the stripe.

"It's a bit like a skating track," said Rachel, landing beside her.

"Yes, and it'll take us wherever we want to go," said Rita. "Just skate forwards. The magic will do the rest."

Smiling broadly, the three fairies pushed forwards. The shooting star instantly sped up, dragging its rainbow tail behind it. Rachel felt her hair flying out behind her as they zoomed across the sky. The star crackled and burned. Then, with a fizz and a flare, it burned away. The fairies were hovering above the city stadium in the park, where the roller derby was in full swing.

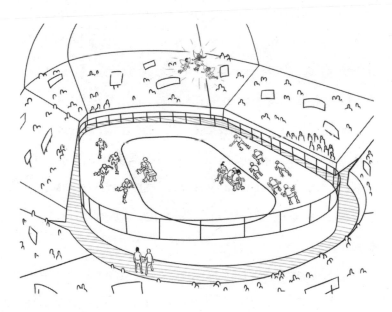

"I don't know where to look first," said Rachel. "It's incredible."

The seats were packed with cheering fans, and the rollerskating rink was enormous. The judges' desk was at the front, and there were three people wearing Olympic Scouts T-shirts in the seats behind them. Many different teams of rollerskaters were whizzing around. One team was dressed in red and black stripes, with a picture of a cat on their T-shirts. Another team was all in pink, with lollipops printed on their vest tops. There were skaters in yellow, blue, orange and every other colour of the rainbow.

"What are they all doing?" Kirsty asked.

"It looks like a practice session for the teams," said Rita. "These are some of the

best rollerskaters in the world."

At that moment, one of the cat team stumbled and fell sideways. She landed on her bottom with a bump.

"Hey, he pushed me," she exclaimed,

pointing to a new skater in the rink.

"It's the goblin!" cried Rachel.

The goblin just laughed and stuck out his tongue at the skater he had pushed. He was wearing a sparkly green skating helmet. He whizzed around the track faster and faster. Then he jumped into the air, did a full turn and landed perfectly.

"He's really good," said Kirsty.

"Yes, but he's a fraud," said Rita. "He isn't good at rollerskating because he has worked hard and practised. He's good because he cheated."

One by one, the other groups were moving to the side of the rink. The goblin was hogging all the space. Soon, all eyes were on him.

"Well, this is a surprise," boomed the announcer. "An unknown skater is astonishing the crowds. World champion Cara White is here all week, and her first performance is tonight. I wonder if this mystery rollerskater will be the next world champion!"

Rita pointed to a young woman who was watching from the rinkside.

"That's Cara White," she told Rachel and Kirsty. "She's incredible. I hope you get the chance to watch her skate."

"She doesn't look very happy," said Rachel.

"You're right," said Rita with a worried

47

frown. "If I turn you back into human beings, will you try to find out what's wrong?"

The fairies nodded, and they all fluttered down to hide underneath a bench behind Cara. With a wave of Rita's wand, Rachel and Kirsty were girls again. They scrambled out from under the bench and went over to Cara. Rita stayed under the bench to watch the goblin.

"Hello," said Kirsty. "Is it OK if we join you for a bit?"

"Sure," said Cara with a smile. "I was just watching the new skater. He's superb."

"Are you looking forward to performing?" Rachel asked.

Cara bit her lip anxiously and turned

to look at them.

"Not really," she said. "I feel so clumsy all of a sudden, and I can't find my lucky skates."

Rachel and Kirsty exchanged a worried look.

"Where did you last see them?" asked Kirsty.

"They were right here," said Cara, taking off her rings. "I can't understand where they've gone. The funny thing is, they look exactly like the ones that superb skater is wearing. But no one would steal another person's skates."

"I wouldn't be so sure about that," muttered Rachel under her breath. She felt certain that the goblin had taken the skates. Cara took off her earrings and necklace and sighed. At that moment, Rita popped up from behind the bench.

"Why are you taking off your jewellery?" asked Kirsty, hoping to distract Cara.

"That's one of the rules of roller derby," said Cara. "No one is allowed to wear jewellery."

She didn't notice
Rita fly over to
Rachel and hide
under her hair.

"The goblin is
causing trouble,"
she whispered. "We
must stop him."

Rachel nodded.

"We have to go now," she said to Cara.
"It was nice to meet you. Good luck with
your performance."

"I hope you find your lucky skates,"
added Kirsty.

Chapter Five
Olympic Dreams

The goblin was no longer in the rink.

"What's going on?" Rachel asked.
"Where is he?"

"He was getting cheers and claps at first," said Rita. "He was doing lots of amazing tricks and some really incredible skating. But then the crowd noticed that he was shoving the other skaters and tripping them up. Rollerskating is a friendly sport. The crowd started to boo and shout 'Shame!', so the goblin stomped off in a huff."

The girls hurried out of the stadium and saw the goblin skating down a path into the park. As they watched, he splashed through a muddy puddle, jumped over a wooden bench and landed in a patch of soggy grass. Then he picked his way back to the bench and sat down, looking miserable.

"Let's go and talk to him," said Kirsty.

They ran down the path and sat down on either side of the goblin. He looked up and glared at them.

"Oh no, not you," he squawked. "What do you want?"

"We just want to talk to you," said Rachel. "You're wearing some things that don't belong to you, and we want you to give them back."

"That's not true!" the goblin shouted. "Go away!"

"Cara looked really sad about her missing skates," said Kirsty.

"Then she shouldn't have left them lying about," said the goblin in a sulky voice. "Finders keepers, losers weepers."

"Nonsense," said Rita, peeping out from underneath Rachel's hair. "You stole those skates from Cara, just like you took the bracelet from me. Give it back."

"Shan't," said the goblin, sticking out his tongue at her. "Stupid fairy."

"It isn't nice to call people names," Rita replied.

"Oh yes it is," said the goblin. "Calling people names is very nice and I like it a lot. So there."

He folded his arms, blew a raspberry at her and turned his face away. Rita was upset, but Kirsty had an idea.

"Sometimes people are unkind because they feel sad or scared," she said. "Goblin, are you upset about something?"

The goblin gave a loud sniff.

"Can we help you?" asked Rachel in a gentle voice.

"I've tried wishing myself home in my hut in Goblin Grotto, but it doesn't work," the goblin muttered. "I'm hungry and I just want to go home."

"I can send you home and give you food," said Rita. "Just give us Cara's skates and my bracelet, and I'll use my magic to transport you to the goblin village."

The goblin stared at her for a moment.

"Really?" he whispered.

"Yes," said Rachel, Kirsty and Rita together.

Then a sly look passed over the goblin's face.

"Never trust a fairy," he said. "That's one of the goblin rules. I'm not giving you any of my things. I'll go back and do some more skating."

Suddenly, a wonderful idea popped into Rachel's head.

"Maybe there's a way that we can get him to take the skates and bracelet off," she whispered.

"What are you whispering about?" the goblin snapped.

"I was just thinking about the Olympic Scouts," said Rachel.

"The what?" said the goblin rudely.

"The Olympic Scouts," Rachel repeated. "They watch sports to find the very best teams to compete in the Olympic Games. You have to be very special to be chosen. They might pick you – if you looked smart enough. Olympic champions always have to look their best."

The goblin looked down at his goblin-skirt and frowned.

"I suppose I could add some sequins,"

he muttered. "Perhaps a few feathers. How about a tutu?"

"I think we can do better than that," said Rachel. "I'm sure Rita would magic you up a perfect new outfit. You'll need to get cleaned up first, though. That muddy puddle splashed you all over."

"There's a shower block in the stadium," said Kirsty. "I saw it when we were chasing after you. Come on, we'll show you where it is."

Chapter Six
Playing by the Rules

A few minutes later, Rachel and Kirsty were outside a shower cubicle. Rachel was sitting on Kirsty's shoulders.

"Catch!" yelled the goblin.

His goblin-skirt flew over the door of the cubicle, followed by his green helmet. Next, Cara's rollerskates were hurled over.

"Yes!" said Rachel in a whisper. "We got them!"

Rita tapped the skates with her wand and all the speckles of mud disappeared.

"Thank goodness," said Kirsty. "Now we can return these to Cara before her performance starts."

Rita nodded, and the skates vanished in a twinkle of fairy dust.

"Cara will be so happy," said Rachel.

"But her lucky skates won't help if the goblin still has my bracelet," said Rita. "It's bound to be a disaster."

They heard the goblin turn the shower on and start to sing.

"I thought your magic was just for after-school sports," said Rachel. "Why is it affecting the roller derby?"

"Because lots of these teams started off as after-school clubs," said Rita with a sigh. "Cara first put on a pair of rollerskates at a leisure-centre club just like yours. My magic affects them all."

The shower stopped, and Rita waved her wand again. A green sparkly jumpsuit appeared over the shower cubicle door.

"Gorgeous!" said the goblin, grabbing the jumpsuit and pulling it on. "I look gorgeous."

He opened the door and pranced
out. Rita pointed her wand again
and matching rollerskates appeared
on his feet. He spun around in a
graceful pirouette. The magical bracelet
glimmered on his wrist.

"How do I look?" he asked.

Just then, Kirsty had a wonderful idea.

"Almost perfect," she said. "There's just one thing. The Olympic Scouts will be checking to make sure you've followed all the rules, and there's one thing that's wrong. Rita, can you magic up a copy of the rules?"

With a flick of Rita's wand, a golden scroll appeared in the air. The list of roller derby rules was written in silver letters. Kirsty pointed at rule number three.

"*No jewellery to be worn in the rink*," she read aloud. "Oh dear, what can we do?"

"Easy peasy!" shouted the goblin.

He tugged the bracelet off his wrist and flung it to the floor. Rita swooped down with a cry of happiness. As soon as she touched her magical bracelet, it shrank to fairy size.

The goblin barely noticed. He was too

busy thinking about the scouts.

"They'll pick me and I'll be famous,"
he said in a boastful voice. "I'll be on TV
and Jack Frost will have to bow to me
and call me 'sir'."

Wobbling, he skated out of the shower
room and headed towards the rink.
Rachel and Kirsty flung their arms
around each other and jumped around,
laughing.

"The goblin might not get picked
without the help of the bracelet," said
Kirsty. "But I hope he has fun trying!"

"Now I will send you back to the
leisure centre," said Rita with a smile.
"I think it's time for you to do some
skating of your own. Thank you for all
your help today. Without you, I would
still be trying to get the goblins to leave

the Fairyland Skatepark. You've been wonderful."

"We enjoyed every minute," said Rachel. "And now we only have one bracelet left to find."

"I'm sure Callie will be along to ask for your help soon," said Rita. "In the meantime, have fun skating! Liz is a great teacher. Goodbye, and thank you again!"

Rachel and Kirsty felt themselves being whisked into the air. It felt as if they had turned into fairy dust for a moment. Then they blinked, and they were back in the rollerskating hall at the Cool Kids Leisure Centre.

"There you are," Liz said to Rachel and Kirsty. "And I see you found the kneepads. Brilliant! Put on your skates – we're about to learn about how to pick

up speed using the crossover."

"I enjoyed that adventure so much," said Kirsty. "The roller derby looks amazing too. Maybe we should ask our parents if we can go and see it together one day this week."

"Great idea," said Rachel. "I'd love to see Cara perform in her lucky skates."

"We need to get our skates on if we're going to enjoy the rest of this class," said Kirsty with a grin. "Let's go!"

The End

Now it's time for Kirsty and
Rachel to help ...

Callie the Climbing Fairy

Read on for a sneak peek ...

"I can't believe that we've tried out
nearly all the after-school clubs," said
Kirsty Tate with a sigh.

She and her best friend Rachel Walker
had already been to three taster classes.
They had shared an exciting adventure
in each one, because Jack Frost had
stolen the four magical bracelets that
belonged to the After School Sports
Fairies. He wanted to shut the Cool
Kids Leisure Centre down and exercise
in private so that he could beat his sister
Jilly Chilly at arm-wrestling. Rachel
and Kirsty had promised to help get the

fairies' bracelets back.

"It's been brilliant," said Rachel. "Now there's just enough time for one more try-out."

"Ready for the climbing club?" asked a voice behind them.

It was Lucy, the young woman who was organising the trial classes. She ticked off their names on her list.

"The climbing wall is through there," she said, pointing to a set of double doors. "The instructor is called Mitchell. Have fun!"

As soon as the girls were in the climbing room, a young man bounded over to them.

"Hi, I'm Mitchell," he said. "No experience of climbing? No problem. You can start off with bouldering, so you won't need a harness. You'll stay close to the ground."

He showed them the colour-coded paths across the wall. Rachel noticed two redheaded girls halfway up.

"Why aren't they moving?" she asked. Mitchell frowned.

"They look scared," he said. "They told me they had climbed before. They're sisters." He cupped his hands around his mouth. "Don't panic, Amy and Fee, just make your way down slowly."

"We can't," said the bigger girl, Amy, in a shaky voice. "We're too dizzy to move."

The smaller sister, Fee, had squeezed her eyes shut.

"No worries," said Mitchell. "Freddy's right next to you. He'll give you a hand."

"Mitchell, I'm too high up," wailed the

boy. "I'm afraid."

"But Freddy's been climbing for years," Mitchell murmured to himself. "I'll have to go up."

He started to pull on a harness, but the straps got tangled around his legs.

Read **Callie the Climbing Fairy** to find out what adventures are in store for Kirsty and Rachel!

Read the brand-new series
from Daisy Meadows…

Ride. Dream. Believe.

Meet best friends Aisha and Emily
and journey to the secret world of
Unicorn Valley!

RAINBOW magic

Calling all parents, carers and teachers!
The Rainbow Magic fairies are here to help
your child enter the magical world of reading.
Whatever reading stage they are at, there's
a Rainbow Magic book for everyone!
Here is Lydia the Reading Fairy's guide to
supporting your child's journey at all levels.